GOOD-BYE
hello

GOOD-BYE
hello

by BARBARA SHOOK HAZEN
illustrated by MICHAEL BRYANT

ATHENEUM BOOKS FOR YOUNG READERS

We're moving, so I
have to say good-bye.
Good-bye for good, old neighborhood.

Good-bye, swings. Good-bye, park.
Good-bye, corner Mini-Mart.

Good-bye, sidewalk. Good-bye, street.
Good-bye, McBurger's for a treat.

Good-bye, pigeon. Good-bye, tree.
Good-bye, cat that follows me.

Good-bye, doorman at the door.
I won't come through here anymore.

Good-bye, secret hiding spot.
I'll miss you an awful lot.

Good-bye, my room most of all,
with all my drawings on the wall.
Good-bye, bed that got too small.

Good-bye, toy shelves.
Good-bye, rocks.
Good-bye, baby books and blocks,

But not to you, Fuzzy Bear.
How did you end up in there?

Good-bye, neighbors that I know,
the Shooks above, the Changs below,
and Mrs. McGrady, the cookie lady.

Good-bye, Jamie.
That's when I start to cry
and hate good-bye.

I'm sad awhile after we go,
until it's time to say hello.

Hello, brand-new neighborhood
with a Pizza Pit and a Toys Are Good.

Hello, new park with a pond
and a great big hill for sledding on.

Hello, yard. Hello, tree.

You're just the perfect size for me.

Hello, squirrel. Don't run away.

Maybe we'll be friends someday.

Hello, mailbox with our name.

Hello, rooms that *aren't* the same.

Hello, walls. Hello, staircase.
Hello, new secret hiding place.

Hello, my new room upstairs.
Hello, new bed; hello, old chairs.

Hello, window. Hello, view—
There's a bird's nest and some people, too.

Hello, new neighbors at the door.
Hello, I'm Terry. Let's explore.

Hello, attic. Hello, drum.
Hello, tent and aquarium.

Hello, boxes with all sorts
of things so we can make a fort.

Hello, Jamie, guess what!
I miss you. But I like it here a lot,
and I can't wait for you to come.

The three of us will really have fun.

Atheneum Books for Young Readers
An imprint of Simon & Schuster Children's Publishing Division
1230 Avenue of the Americas
New York, New York 10022

The text of this book is set in Primer.
The illustrations are rendered in watercolors.
First edition
Printed in the United States of America

10   9   8   7   6   5   4   3   2   1

Library of Congress Cataloging-in-Publication Data

Hazen, Barbara Shook.
    Good-bye/Hello/by Barbara Shook Hazen.
        p.   cm.
    Summary: For all the sadness in "good-byes," there are
corresponding happy moments in "hellos," as an urban child moves to
a suburban neighborhood.
    ISBN 0–689–31665–8
    [1. Moving, Household—Fiction.]   I. Title.
PZ7.H314975Gm   1995
[E]—dc20   91–39591